Siege!

by

Ann Jungman

Illustrated by Alan Marks

HAMPSHIRE
COUNTY LIBRARY
H 00 2132172
Peters 08-Jun-06
JF £4.99
9781842994078
1842994077
WITHDRAWN

You do not need to read this page – just get on with the book!

First published in 2006 in Great Britain by
Barrington Stoke Ltd
www.barringtonstoke.co.uk

This edition based on *Siege!* published by
Barrington Stoke in 2005

Copyright © 2006 Ann Jungman
Illustrations © Alan Marks

The moral right of the author has been asserted in accordance with the Copyright, Designs and Patents Act 1988

ISBN 1-842994-07-7
13 digit ISBN 978-1-84299-407-8

Printed in Great Britain by Bell & Bain Ltd

Meet The Author – Ann Jungman

What is your favourite animal?
Wolf
What is your favourite boy's name?
Guy
What is your favourite girl's name?
Abigail
What is your favourite food?
Beef stroganoff
What is your favourite music?
Bob Dylan
What is your favourite hobby?
Cinema and cooking

Meet The Illustrator – Alan Marks

What is your favourite animal?
Snow leopard
What is your favourite boy's name?
Thomas
What is your favourite girl's name?
Kate
What is your favourite food?
Oysters
What is your favourite music?
Mozart
What is your favourite hobby?
Cooking

For Penny and Jamie and
in memory of Paul

Contents

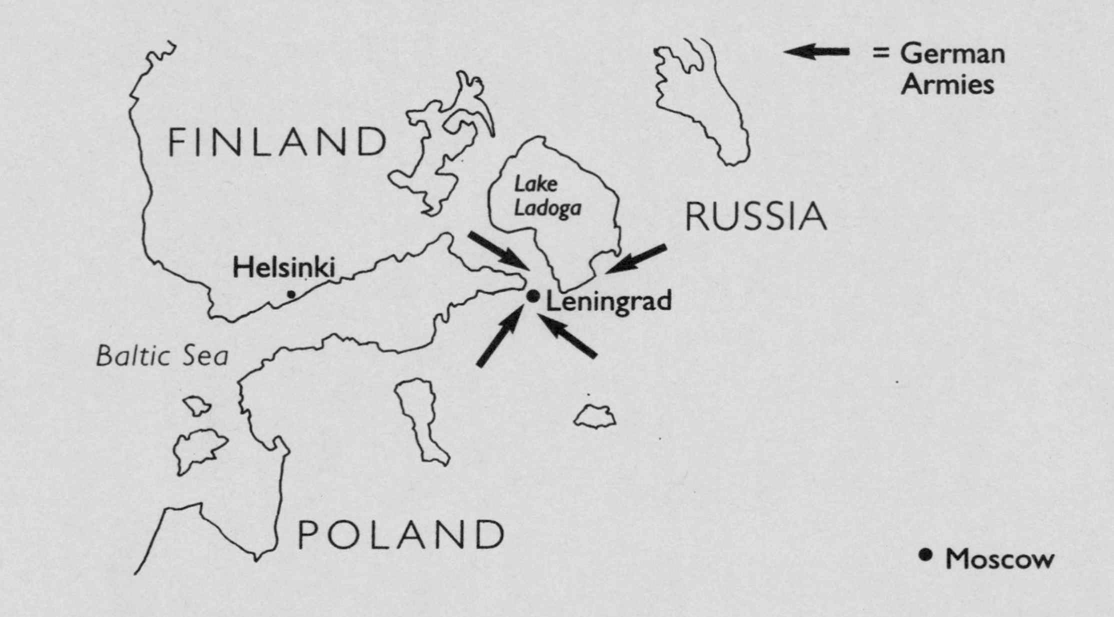
= German Armies
FINLAND
Lake Ladoga
RUSSIA
Helsinki
Leningrad
Baltic Sea
POLAND
Moscow

Chapter 1
Digging

Ivan looked out of the window. He wished he was still on holiday. He loved to fish in the river and to pick berries. Ivan didn't like school very much.

All at once, the door of the class-room was flung open and the head-master walked in. He was in a hurry.

"All of you, get into the trucks outside," he yelled. "Russia needs you."

All the boys looked at one another. They were puzzled.

"What does he mean?" asked one.

"No talking," snapped the head-master. "Into the trucks and do as you are told."

The boys drove along the wide streets of Leningrad. *What a fine city this is,* Ivan thought. There was a lot of traffic on the roads that day. Truck after truck full of students and school children was driving down the streets that were so empty most of the time. What did this mean?

Soon they'd left the city behind and were out in the country. The truck came to a sudden stop.

“Everyone out,” yelled their teacher. As the boys jumped down from the lorry, a Russian soldier came up to them.

“Everyone grab one of those spades and follow me!” he yelled. “Move it!”

Ivan ran after him.

“What’s this all about?” he panted. “What are we doing out here?”

“Didn’t they tell you?” asked the soldier.

Ivan shook his head. “No-one knows,” he said.

“Hitler has invaded Russia,” the soldier said and spat on the side of the road. “The Germans have crossed our border like robbers in the night. There was no warning. They never told us we were at war. They just began to bomb and kill us.”

"But Comrade Stalin, our great leader, made a pact with Hitler. It said that we wouldn't invade Germany and they wouldn't invade us," said Ivan.

"For pigs like Hitler a scrap of paper doesn't mean a thing. He makes a pact when he feels like it and then he tears it up later. All right, boys! Stop here and start to dig."

Ivan took a deep breath and started to dig. There were others digging all around him. Most were young but some older people were there as well, all busy with their spades.

"What are we digging?" asked a girl.

"Tank traps," the soldier said in a grim voice. "Big trenches that the German tanks won't be able to cross."

“Tanks?” said Ivan. “But the Germans will never get this far, will they? We’re hundreds of miles from the border.”

“Yes, well, better safe than sorry,” the soldier went on. “We didn’t know they were going to make war on us. Our armies aren’t ready and may not be able to stop the Germans. So they may easily get as far as this. We need to be ready for them. Dig in groups of ten and don’t waste your breath talking. Just keep on digging.”

Ivan and the others dug and dug. Soon they were damp with the heat and had big blisters on their hands.

All around them other groups were working as hard as they were. They weren’t talking or looking around but just kept on at the job. Ivan looked up and was amazed to see his sister Varya with a spade in her hand.

Ivan has no idea
how bad things are

Varya, his stuck-up sister was doing something useful with her hands for once. Varya was a prize pupil at the most famous music school in Leningrad. She played the piano and always had to keep her hands dry and soft. She could never even wash up a cup. Ivan grinned. *Oh well,* he thought, *this war isn't all bad.*

"Hey, Varya," he yelled. "What are you doing here? You'll have to soak your hands for at least six hours after this."

"Don't talk rot," his sister yelled back. She was angry. "All Russians have got to help in any way they can. Look – even my teacher is here, digging like the rest of us."

Ivan gasped. Varya's teacher was the most famous composer and pianist in all of Russia and here he was with a spade. This was not at all the same as playing the piano. Things must be bad.

Chapter 2
Alone

They drove back to Leningrad as the sun was setting. Water glinted in the canals. You were never far from water in Leningrad. The city had been built on marshes and you could never forget it. The Baltic Sea was on one side and huge Lake Ladoga on the other.

Ivan and Varya walked slowly up the steps of their flat. They were worn out and dirty and had blisters all over their hands. At the top of the stairs stood their dad in his army uniform.

"I'm so glad you're here," he called to them. "I've been waiting for you. I have to go back to the army. I didn't want to go without saying good-bye."

Varya's face went pale.

"Will you be gone a long time?" Ivan asked. He was worried.

"No, of course not," his dad said. "We'll have those Germans back across the border in no time."

That won't happen, thought Ivan. How often had he heard his dad talking softly to his mum at night? He had said that Comrade Stalin had got rid of all the best generals.

"As soon as someone shows he's good or his men like him, Stalin gets jealous and has him shot," his dad had said.

"Wish me luck, then," said his dad and they held onto each other hard in a big hug.

“Don’t look so upset. The Germans won’t win. If we can hold out till winter, there are two great generals waiting for Hitler and his armies.”

Ivan gave a grin. “You mean General Frost-bite and General Hunger will get them.”

“That’s right, Ivan, and don’t you forget it. We Russians know how to deal with the cold in a way others don’t. Just remember how we’ve always got rid of invaders in the past. All those armies that tried to take over Russia, the French, the Germans, they’ve all had to turn back. No-one can beat us on Russian soil – it may take time but we’ll win in the end. Just think about that and hold onto it, even if things look grim. Now come on, I want to take a photo of my family, so I can see you when I’m far away.”

Ivan and Varya sat with their mum and little Sasha while their dad took some photos. Two-year-old Sasha made everyone smile by pulling his mum's hair.

"Now let me take one of you, Dad," cried Ivan, taking the camera from him. "Then we can still see you when *you're* far away, too."

So Ivan took a photo of them all.

Then their dad put on his coat and his fur hat and went to the door. He hugged

and kissed their mum and little Sasha, and then Ivan and Varya.

"I trust you both to look after your mum and Sasha," he said.

"Don't worry, Dad, we will," Ivan told him. Then his dad ran down the stairs and jumped into a waiting truck.

They all rushed to the window to wave to him.

"Do you think we'll ever see him again?" their mum said softly and kissed Sasha on the top of his head.

"Of course we will," yelled Varya. "We will, I know we will and we'll crush that horrid Hitler, too."

"I do hope you're right," said her mum with a sigh. "Now, I'm sorry but you two are going to have to look after Sasha tonight.

I'm on night duty. All doctors have to report to the hospital. There's some food in the kitchen. I'll be back to look after Sasha in the morning, before you go to school."

After she left, Varya and Ivan looked at each other.

"What a day," Varya said. "First we dig trenches all day and then both our parents have to go off and leave us here."

"I know," said Ivan. "It all feels very odd. But something tells me it's going to get even more grim."

Chapter 3
The Siege

Things moved very fast in the next few weeks. German planes often flew low over Leningrad dropping bombs. German guns kept shelling the city. The noise was awful. Ivan and Varya didn't see their mum much. She was busy at the hospital. She had to look after the hundreds of soldiers who had been hurt in the war. Most nights she slept at work, if she got any sleep at all. Soon there was no more school and their old life was gone.

One day their mum came home, pale and worn out.

"There's going to be a siege. Hitler's made up his mind to take the city," she said.

"A siege!" cried Ivan. "But sieges are things of long ago. They belong to the days of battering rams, when they poured boiling oil from the city walls. That's not modern war."

"Well, the Germans are going to set up camp all round Leningrad so we all die of hunger," their mum told him grimly.

"No way," cried Ivan. "They'll never win. I'd rather die than give in to them."

"Me too," said Varya.

"Sasha too," said their little brother, nodding.

They all smiled, glad to find something to smile about.

"Children, you must think hard about what I am going to say," said their mum. "Most of the children are being taken out of

Leningrad. I can't go. They need all the doctors to stay here. But you *could* go. I've got places for you on a truck."

"What about Sasha?" asked Ivan.

"You must take him too," said their mum. She sounded worn out.

"We can't leave you here all alone. We must stick by you, Mum. I'm staying with you. Varya can take Sasha in the truck."

"If you think I'm going and leaving you here, you're wrong," snapped Varya. "I could have gone with my piano teacher. He begged me to go with him, but I said no. I'm not going now, just because you asked me to take Sasha."

"Please, Varya," begged her mum.

"No, Ivan and I will look after Sasha and fight for our city if we have to."

"Things will get very bad," their mum told them. "If they bomb the power stations there will be no heat. There is very little food left and the bombing and shelling will get worse."

"We've made up our minds, Mum. There's no more to say," smiled Ivan. "Now, you look worn out. Let me make you a cup of tea and then you must sleep for a bit."

Their mum began to smile.

All at once, my children have grown up. It's a shock but a nice one, she thought.

Their mum was right. Things did get worse. Winter came and it was freezing cold. Just as she said, the power stations were bombed and there was no light and no heat. Life was now all about staying alive.

Varya found a few candles for light and Ivan went out and took bits of wood from bombed houses. Everyone else was doing the same and Ivan got into lots of fights.

One freezing night Varya was hugging a cold and sad Sasha, "We'd better burn some of Dad's books," she said.

"Varya, are you mad? Dad would never forgive you."

"Of course he would. Look at Sasha. He's so cold. Go and get some books, the big thick ones. They'll burn well and not too fast. And while you're at it, bring some of my music. We'll burn that too, to warm us up a bit."

"But, Varya, your music is the most important thing in your life."

"The most important thing in my life is that we all stay alive. You must do what I say. I'll tell Dad why we had to burn his books when the war is over."

The war has changed Varya, thought Ivan, looking at her.

"I remember when a broken finger nail seemed like the worst thing in the world to you," he said. "I used to think you were a spoilt brat. I was wrong."

Varya smiled.

They've bombed the
food ware-house

That night Ivan stood on the roof of their block of flats and watched out for fire-bombs. Everyone from the flats took it in turns to keep watch. Some planes flew low above the houses and a bomb fell. Ivan rushed to get it and then dropped it in a bucket of water. He walked up and down stamping his feet and rubbing his hands to keep them warm. He tried not to think about how hungry he was.

I hate all Germans, he thought. *If it wasn't for them our family would be together, and I wouldn't be freezing cold and hungry and scared. I hate every German in the world. I want to kill as many as I can.*

Then Ivan smelled something fantastic. It wasn't the smell he now knew so well of burning and bombs. Something smelled very good. Then he saw a huge fire burning in the middle of the city.

Ivan saw that the main food ware-house was on fire. That was where most of the food in Leningrad was kept. The food ware-house had been bombed. The fantastic smell made his hunger even worse. Ivan knew it was the last of the city's store of food for the winter going up in flames.

Now we'll starve, as well as freeze, thought Ivan grimly. Another fire-bomb dropped and Ivan picked it up and threw it into the bucket of water. *But we won't give in. No, we'll never give in.*

Chapter 4
Hunger

The weeks passed and nothing got any better. After the bombing of the food store there was less and less to eat.

"I'm hungry all the time," moaned Ivan.

"Everyone is," snapped his sister. "A slice of bread a day is too little for anyone."

"It isn't even proper bread," Ivan went on. "It's got sawdust and mice droppings in it. No-one cares as long as we get *something*."

"We get as much as anyone else," Varya told him. "Only the workers in the factories and the soldiers get more than us."

Sasha began to cry. "Sasha hungry," he moaned.

Ivan and Varya looked at one another. Varya picked Sasha up and hugged him.

She was now so weak and hungry that she could hardly lift him at all.

"I'm hungry!" Sasha went on moaning.

"Strip the wall-paper off the wall," Varya told Ivan.

"Why, Varya? Even if we put it in the stove it'll only burn for a moment."

"We're not going to burn it. We need to boil it up to make some soup for Sasha. I've heard there's goodness in the glue."

"Glue soup," sniffed Ivan. "It sounds awful."

"Don't make a fuss, Ivan," his sister said. "It might save our lives. Go and make up a fire with Mum's medical books and I'll take this pot and go up onto the roof. I'll get some snow and melt it to make the glue soup."

When Varya came back with the snow, she said, "Your belt, Ivan. I need it for the soup."

"You can't have my belt. My trousers will fall down."

"Use this bit of string to keep your trousers up. I need your belt. We'll boil that too, there may be some fat in it."

That night they all sat round and ate the soup Varya had made. She put in their last onion as well. They dipped their bread into the soup and ate it all up. They began to feel a bit better. Sasha stopped crying and fell asleep. Ivan tried not to think of

his mum's pork and roast potatoes. He hadn't eaten any good food for a long time.

"The people upstairs have been eating rats and cats," Ivan told Varya.

"I know, but they still look skinny and ill," Varya said.

Ivan nodded. "We all look skinny and ill," he said. "I'm on fire duty on the roof again tonight. Shall I go and look for some wood before I go?"

"Yes, please. You can take the sledge."

So Ivan went out into their street but it didn't look the same any more. Once there had been tall, grand houses and shops. Now there were broken walls and holes in the road. There were no trams or cars. All was silent. Lying here and there were the bodies of people who had died of hunger in the

I don't care if it's wrong - we must stay alive

streets as they went looking for food. One boy had fallen over, dead, with a pile of wood beside him. Ivan looked in the boy's pockets for his ration book and then picked up the wood. You could be killed for taking a ration book but Ivan didn't care. All he wanted was to help poor little Sasha.

As he went home along the freezing street, Ivan hoped that someone would come and take the dead bodies away. Now that there were so many deaths, the bodies often just lay where they fell for days.

It's amazing, Ivan thought. *Any other city would have given in but we just keep on going, no matter how many people die.*

Chapter 5
Sasha

Ivan was just going up the stairs with the wood when a few lights went on.

Lighting, thought Ivan. *I'd forgotten what it was like.* Slowly he pushed open the door of their flat.

"I got us wood," Ivan told Varya. "I found it by a dead boy."

“Did you take his ration book?” asked Varya in a stern voice.

“Yes,” said Ivan. “I don’t care! If it means helping Sasha, I’ll do anything.”

“Give it to me,” Varya said. Ivan handed it to her. Varya threw it into the fire and said grimly, “Don’t ever do that again, Ivan. I need you. No more crazy risks.”

“Why are the lights on?” asked Ivan.

“Someone told me that they’ve been trying all day to get it to work so that we can all listen to the radio and hear the new music that my teacher, Shostakovich, has written about us.”

“Your old teacher has written some music about us?” asked Ivan.

“Yes. It will tell the world how brave we are to hold out in this siege. The whole of

Russia will have their radios on tonight and now we can hear the music, too."

Varya filled the stove with wood and turned on the radio. The three children sat close together. They put on all the clothes they had to keep warm.

"This is the first time this new work has been played," said the voice on the radio. "It's by the great Shostakovich himself. This music has been written for the brave people of Leningrad. People of Leningrad, all of Russia knows how brave you are – this music is for you."

As the radio played the children could hear it all in the music, the snow, the frost, the shelling and the bombs. They could hear walls crashing to the ground, but they could also hear how brave the people of Leningrad were – a city that would not give in.

"If you had left when you had the chance, Varya," Ivan said, "you could be playing that music now. Do you ever wish you'd gone?"

"No," said Varya. "No, how could I have left you all? I am only sad that I can't play that fantastic music."

I hate this war so much
We did all we could for him

"Sasha liked the music too," Ivan went on. "Look – he's fast asleep."

Varya smiled down at the child and put a hand on his pale cheek. Then she stopped.

"Ivan, Sasha is cold as ice."

Ivan picked Sasha up. His body was limp and his head flopped back.

"He's dead," said Ivan in a shaky voice. "He's died, Varya."

"Poor little Sasha," sobbed Varya. "He was so hungry and cold." The two of them held onto each other and cried and cried.

Chapter 6
Captured

"We must tell Mum," said Varya.

"We can't," said Ivan. "How can we get a message to her? Nothing works any more. There are no trams, nothing. And we can't walk to the hospital. It's too far, we're too weak and it's too risky. The bombs are falling all the time. What are we going to do with Sasha's body? There's no-one left to come and take the bodies away and bury them."

"Even if there was," said Varya grimly, "I don't want him to be buried in this broken city that is so full of pain and anger. I want our Sasha to be somewhere where there is peace and beauty."

"There's nowhere like that any more in Leningrad," said Ivan. "But if we took him to our old summer house outside the city, then we could bury his body there, under the tree where he loved to play."

"Maybe we could take him there at night," Varya said. "The summer house is in no-man's land. It lies between us and the German army and it's close by."

"But how can we get out of the city? No-one's allowed to be out at night," Ivan said.

"Who'd see us?" said Varya. "There's not many people left, so many are sick or dead. No-one would bother."

That night the two set off. They pulled Sasha's small body on the sledge. They'd wrapped him up in his old blanket. They could not walk fast because they felt so weak. At the end of a street they saw a Russian soldier.

"We'll slip through that empty warehouse," said Ivan, "then he won't see us."

They waited until the guard moved on and then crept out towards the edge of the city. They got to the country at last and they found their summer house. It was no longer standing. It had been bombed.

"Look," said Varya, "Sasha's tree is still there. That's where we'll bury him." She picked up his small body and they began to walk over to the tree.

Just then, they heard the tramping of boots. A torch shone in their faces.

"Hands up!" came a harsh voice. There were five German soldiers, all pointing their guns at the two children. Ivan put both his hands up but Varya couldn't because she was still holding Sasha.

One soldier pressed his gun into Varya's back but she still wouldn't drop Sasha.

"What have you got there?" yelled one of the soldiers in German. "Is that a bomb?"

Ivan didn't understand a word but Varya replied in German.

"No, this isn't a bomb. It's our baby brother. He's dead and we wanted to bury him under the tree where he liked to play. This used to be our summer house."

"They must be spies," said one of the Germans. "The girl speaks German."

"Yes, I speak German," said Varya, "because I'm a music student. I had to learn German so that I could sing German songs."

Ivan was shaking with fear. How could Varya stay so calm and tell the German officer what he wanted to know?

“Show me your bundle,” ordered the German.

Without a word, Varya handed him the bundle.

“They’re telling the truth,” said the soldier. “There’s a little boy in here and he’s dead.”

This could have been my boy

Chapter 7
The Enemy

"How did the child die?" asked one of the soldiers.

"We don't know," Varya told them. "We've been so cold and there's no food. We are all weak and ill. There are thousands, tens of thousands like him."

"Where do you want to bury your brother?" asked a soldier.

"There, under that tree where he used to play. We used to have all our summer holidays here."

"What's going on?" hissed Ivan, who was still very scared. "Are they going to shoot us?"

"I don't think so," Varya told him.

The German soldiers talked together. Then one of them walked over to Varya and Ivan. He looked as if he was the officer in charge.

"We are very sad about your brother," the officer said. "We are not happy that children are getting killed and dying like that. We would like to help you bury him out here."

"They want to help us," Varya told Ivan. "They say they're upset that a little boy like Sasha died because of the siege."

"Then why don't they lift the siege and go home?" yelled Ivan in an angry voice.

"What's he saying?" the officer asked Varya.

"He says if you're so upset about Sasha, why don't you just go home to Germany?"

"You think we don't want to? I have a child just the same age as your dead brother. Maybe my child is dead, too. Germany is being bombed by the British. Do you think I like freezing out here month after month? Most of us are here because we were made to join the German army. If we run away and try to go home, we'll be shot."

Varya looked into the man's blue eyes. She could see he was telling the truth. He and his men hated the war just as much as she and Ivan did. They were longing to go home. And she knew that if any of his men told anyone what he had just said, the officer would be shot. He was a brave man.

"I understand," she told him. "The war is grim for us all."

She turned back to Ivan. "They're going to help us bury Sasha. The officer has a son the same age as Sasha and I think he feels sorry for us and bad about the siege."

Two of the soldiers went away and came back with spades. They dug a hole under Sasha's tree.

"Why did you pick this place to bury him?" asked the officer. "It was crazy of you to leave the city. You're in great danger now."

"When people die in Leningrad there's no-one left to bury them. If they are buried, the bodies are thrown into big pits with all the other dead people. We want to bury Sasha in a place of peace and beauty, where he can feel the wind and hear the birds singing. He loved the woods."

"Would you like us all to sing your brother to sleep as we bury him? Then his spirit can be free and happy in the woods when at last the war is over."

At least Sasha can sleep in peace at last

Varya told Ivan what the officer had said. “They want to sing Sasha to sleep, so that his spirit can rest in peace. What do you think?”

Ivan nodded, “OK. Sasha always loved singing, he’d like that.”

“I’ll sing in German with you,” said Varya to the soldiers. “Ivan will just hum along with us.”

They dug a grave for Sasha and laid his body in it. While two of the soldiers put the earth in over him, the others sang. As they sang, tears ran down Varya’s and Ivan’s faces. When they looked up, they saw that some of the German soldiers were crying, too.

If Germans can cry like that, thought Ivan, *they can’t be all bad.*

Chapter 8
A Surprise

"What are you going to do with us now?" asked Varya. "If you're going to kill us, please bury us next to our brother."

"No more talk of death and killing," said the officer. "Just go back in secret."

All at once, Ivan's legs felt so weak he couldn't stand up any more. He flopped onto the ground. Varya was very weak, too. She sat down next to the tree.

"You're starving, aren't you?" said the officer. He yelled to his men. "Here, all of you, give these children some food."

Soon Ivan and Varya had a bit of bread and sausage to eat. One of the soldiers gave them some hot coffee. Ivan had never tasted anything so good. Slowly he felt his legs getting a little stronger.

"Can you walk back to Leningrad now?" asked the officer.

Ivan nodded. He began to walk away, then he turned round and held out his hand to the officer. "Thank you for helping us," he said. "When this war is over, I hope we can be friends."

Varya told the German officer what Ivan had said. The officer smiled and they shook hands. Then Ivan and Varya walked away. It was just getting light when at last they got back to their flat.

"No-one saw us," said Varya. They fell onto their beds and were asleep at once.

A few hours later Ivan woke up to hear someone banging on the door. He got up to open it. There stood a Russian army officer.

Ivan's heart sank. Had someone found out what they had done the night before? Had someone told on them?

"I have come to speak to Comrade Varya," said the officer loudly.

"She's asleep," Ivan told him.

"Well, when she wakes up tell her she must go to the concert hall."

“How can she? The concert hall was bombed out ages ago.”

“That’s right. It has been bombed but even so we’re going to have a concert. We’re going to play the music Shostakovich wrote for us. We need Varya to play the piano.”

“But she hasn’t played the piano for so long ...”

“No-one’s played any music for a long time but I’ve been told to find everyone in Leningrad who’s still alive and can play. They must all be at the hall by 4 p.m.”

“She’ll be there,” Ivan told him.

I thought I would never see them again!
How are we going to tell her about Sasha?

Chapter 9
The Concert

Varya brushed her hair and put on her best dress. Then she put on her coat and gloves and big boots as well. Then, Ivan and Varya walked through the bombed streets to the concert hall. Outside the hall, they saw their mum. She looked grey and worn out and so thin. The two children ran up to her and hugged and kissed her.

“Sasha?” she asked them. “Where is Sasha?”

Varya and Ivan said nothing.

"I know. He's dead," said their mum in a sad small voice. "Like so many others."

"We did our best, truly we did," Ivan told her.

"I know," said his mum. She was crying now. "I know how much you both loved him."

"We've buried him in the woods near the summer house," Varya told her mum. "That was where he loved to be and where he can hear the birds singing."

"That makes me feel better. Come on, Varya. The other doctors at the hospital said I could come here today to hear you play. Let's go in, my clever child. You play so well."

Inside the bombed hall there were lots of people. Most of them looked pale and thin and only just alive. There were rather few players there and when the conductor came in, Ivan saw that his hands were shaking from cold and hunger.

Most of the people playing were soldiers who'd come in from the fighting for the concert. Some of them had even come from the hospital and had bandages on their legs or heads. They all looked hungry and dirty. Even so, when the concert started, everyone sat up. The music sounded strong and brave. The players put all their hopes and fears into the music. Ivan felt his spirits rise. Before, when he'd gone to hear Varya play the piano, he'd been bored, but this was not the same thing. Here were people, half-dead in a bombed city and still able to make music. Ivan's heart was full of pride for the people of Leningrad.

Chapter 10
The Ice Road

As they sat in the concert hall and the music played, Ivan held his mum's hand. She was crying softly.

Then he felt someone tap him on the back.

"We need more men to defend the city. So many of our men are here at the concert. Can you take a gun and help us?"

Ivan nodded. He gripped his mum's hand before he left.

"I have to go, Mum, they need me to help defend the city."

His mum nodded. "I'm very proud of you. I'm very proud of you and Varya," she said.

Ivan took the gun and went out after the soldier onto the bombed streets.

At last, he thought, *at last I'm going to be able to do my bit to save Leningrad. And I'm going to kill as many of those Germans as I can.*

But then he thought of the officer who had helped them bury Sasha and the men who had sung him to sleep.

We've got to win this war, he thought. *We must. But after that I'll find those men.*

If we get through this awful war, maybe we can all make a better world.

Ivan went with the soldier into a house and up some stairs.

"See over there," said the soldier, "that's where the Germans are. You must try and shoot as many as you can." Ivan looked out and saw the German army lined up all round Leningrad. Only the lake was still and empty. Nothing moved on the ice.

All at once, far away out on the lake, he saw some trucks moving.

"Look over there, those trucks, what are they doing?" Ivan asked.

The soldier looked out to where Ivan was pointing. He stopped, then he said, "Those trucks are *ours*, boy. They're our trucks and they're bringing us food and guns. Our lads are getting over to us at last."

"How?" asked Ivan.

"They're coming across the frozen lake. We call it the Ice Road. When the ice is thick enough, trucks can drive across it from the far side where there are no German troops. But it's very risky. They're bringing us food and help and they can

take the sick and starving people away. Look, they're coming closer now. You'll see them clearly soon. Trucks, all loaded with food and they're flying the Russian flag."

He put a hand on Ivan's arm. "We're going to win this war. General Frost-bite and General Hunger will really start to attack the Germans now. They can't sit around for ever, not with our winters."

As Ivan watched the trucks driving over the ice, Ivan knew it was true. Leningrad was going to survive. He and Varya and his mum were still alive. Maybe his dad was alive, too.

Leningrad was bombed to bits. Half the people were dead, the houses and shops had gone, but the spirit of the city lived on. *Cities can grow once more from the ashes,* Ivan thought. Leningrad would rise again.

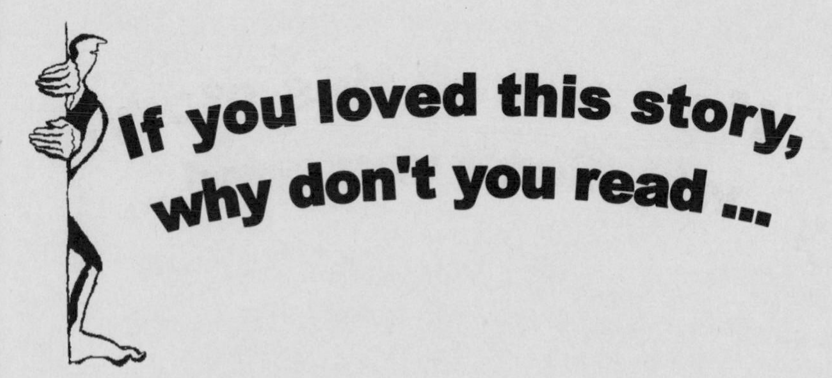

Resistance

by Ann Jungman

Do you ever disagree with your parents? Jan is ashamed when his Dutch father sides with the Germans during the Second World War. Only Elli is his friend. Can Jan find a way to help the Resistance?

4u2read.ok!

You can order this book directly from our website
www.barringtonstoke.co.uk

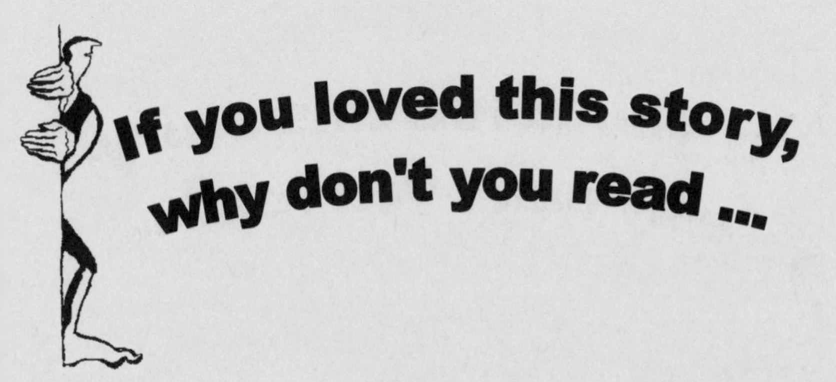

The Secret Room

by Hazel Townson

Adam thinks a school storeroom may hold the clue to a secret room. But to his horror, he finds he has gone back in time – to the Second World War. Adam can see his friend Jade is in terrible danger. But is she in the past or in present? And can Adam save her?

4u2read.ok!

You can order this book directly from our website
www.barringtonstoke.co.uk